Stranger and the General's Wife

by Aubrey McFarren

Illustrated by Jennifer Medeiros ~ Designed by Amy Koch Johnson

IN LOVING MEMORY
Of
An American Hero
First Lieutenant Jonathan P. Brostrom,
United States Army
Killed in action on July 13, 2008 in Afghanistan,
while leading his Airborne Infantry Platoon.

Dedicated with love
to my grandchildren,
Hannah, Megan, Mira, Willie, and
my husband and best friend,
General Freddy,
and to
Stranger and all our beloved pets.

With deep appreciation to my dear
friend, Paula Rieker, who kindly
spent much time proof-reading my story.

"Let everything that has breath praise the LORD!"
Psalm 150:6

This book belongs to

_____

TABLE OF CONTENTS

Chapter One

Abandoned and Afraid

On a very dark night, I was suddenly dropped out of a black pickup truck onto a gravel road. I landed hard on my back right leg as the truck sped off, leaving a cloud of dust behind. I wondered what was happening to me and if the truck would come back.

When I tried to stand, pain shot through my leg, and I let out a loud whine and whimper. I had hoped the man driving the truck was going to keep me as his own dog. He had picked me out at the animal shelter and seemed like a nice guy, but now I was abandoned and afraid. He had obviously decided he did not want a black lab. Maybe he thought I was too big.

Ouch! It hurt when I tried to stand on my leg. I limped to the side of the road where there were large trees. The sky began to rumble with thunder, and lightning made big jagged streaks and illuminated the dark clouds. Then, it began to rain. The drops were falling slowly at first, but about the time I reached the covering of the trees, the rain came down hard. The thunder and lightning scared me, but I felt a little safer under the huge trees with thick branches.

After looking around, I saw a good spot under one of the largest trees. I arranged the fallen leaves with my paw, turned in several circles, laid down being careful not to lie on my hurt leg, and curled up in a ball like a sleeping cat. Somehow, being curled up made me feel even safer.

There was one scraped spot on my leg that was bleeding. I slowly cleaned the wound by licking it with my tongue. The blood had dried on my fur, and I had to pull it out with my teeth. It was painful, but I continued until my fur was clean. The day was not going as I had hoped. I thought I had found a home where a family would love and care for me. Now, I was abandoned and afraid. The wind was blowing hard, and the tree branches swayed back and forth over my head.

I wished the booming thunder and jagged streaks of lightning would stop. My body began to tremble in fear. Then, I curled up tighter and tucked my head under my bushy tail. I was so tired and could not keep my eyes open.

The next morning, I awakened to rays

of sunlight streaming through the trees. Slowly, I raised my head with my nose high in the air and sniffed the surrounding area. The rain had stopped. I did not hear, see, or smell anything unusual. My hurt leg was really stiff and sore, but I stood up slowly while letting my three good legs do the work. Then, I shook myself hard, and the leaves which had been stuck to my fur fell to the ground. There is nothing like a good stretch and shake to start the day, but I could not help wondering what might happen next.

Not knowing if I could walk on three legs but, ready to try, I held up my hurt leg, began to scout around, and hoped that today would be better than yesterday. Perhaps I might find a family who would love me and want me to be their dog. I would not find a family by staying under that tree. It was time to get moving!

Chapter Two

On My Own

Soon, I reached a spot where I could get a better look around. Through the covering of the trees, I could see the road where the man had abandoned me the night before. Puddles had formed from the rain, and I enjoyed a long drink until my thirst was quenched. My stomach began to make growling sounds, reminding me I was hungry. Until then, I had never worried about food. I hoped my natural instincts would take over as I began searching for something to eat.

Smelling the ground, I followed the same path I had taken while looking for a safe spot to sleep. Once I reached the edge of the woods, I paused to check for anything suspicious. All seemed quiet, so I walked cautiously to the road. It was soft and muddy from all the rain. Too bad it had not been soft the day I fell from the truck! Thinking the man might come back to get me, I ignored my growling stomach, laid down on the muddy ground, and watched for a long time. But, there were no signs of a black truck. I would not find food if I stayed in that spot all day, so I decided to start looking for anything I could eat.

Hours and hours went by, and I did not find any food or a place to safely rest. It was getting very hot. The air felt heavy as the moisture from the rain rose from the ground like steam. Just then, I heard a noise and looked in the direction of the sound. I thought it might be the man returning to get me, because the sound I heard was coming from a black truck. As the truck got closer, my tail began to wag, and my heart beat faster. But the truck sped right past me, splattering water and mud on my face. Feeling pretty sad that it was not the man, I decided to find a place to rest until the sun went down, and it got cooler.

In a few minutes, I spied a huge hollow tree trunk which provided a safe place for a much needed nap. As quickly as possible, I made my way there and peered inside to be certain it was empty. Then, I crouched down low to squeeze through the opening. It was cool inside and felt very soothing to my tired, aching body. My hunger did not keep me from falling into a deep sleep.

Sounds of growling awakened me from a deep sleep. Startled, I opened my eyes, lifted my head, and looked outside. Oh no! I saw two dogs snarling at each other with wide-opened eyes. But, then, I realized there were more dogs. All of them were fighting, growling, chasing, and tumbling with each other. One dog was smaller than the others. I was scared!

The bigger dogs began to attack the smaller one. Suddenly, the big dogs saw something moving on the ground and shifted their energies to pursue the newer target. While the larger dogs were busy trying to catch their new prey, the smaller dog was able to sneak away without them noticing. I did not make a sound.

I trembled with fear. What if those dogs decided to look inside the hollow tree trunk? What if they picked up my scent? I wondered if I should try to sneak away by going out the other end of the trunk, but that opening was very narrow. However, it was the only safe way out, so I laid flat on my belly and started to crawl. I still heard the dogs, but they were not growling. Instead, they were busy eating their catch. As I continued crawling, the space became even smaller. If I crawled any farther, I might get stuck, so I stopped. After a while, I no longer heard the dogs, but I still waited and waited.

When night came, there were all sorts of sounds. I remained very quiet and laid my head down between my two front paws. I kept my eyes open to watch for anything that might come inside the other end of the log. Sure enough, a pair of squirrels scurried inside my safe place, but they did not notice me. They would surely make a great meal and, boy, was I hungry! If I started to move, they would hear me and run away before I could catch them. Just then, one of the squirrels started moving toward me, and I thought this might really be an easy catch. Patience was necessary. I knew I had to wait for just the right moment to make my move. The squirrel would have to get really close for me to grab him. His tail began swishing fast; he was sensing something. He stopped and stared straight at me. I knew that was the moment to act so, without hesitating, I raised my paw and slammed it down on the squirrel's tail. Then, I grabbed at him with my other paw. To my great disappointment, he slipped away, alerting the other squirrel as he ran. In a flash, they were both gone! There was no way I could have crawled out of the hollow trunk in time to catch them, so

I was left alone with my empty stomach!
Well, at least it was daylight, and the
four mean dogs seemed to be gone. So, I
decided to crawl to the larger end of the
trunk and squeeze outside.

Chapter Three

The Chase

Another day began, and I still wondered if I might encounter the pack of wild dogs. I hoped to pick up the scent of the squirrels. Guess what? Even before I moved, I saw the squirrels only a few yards away. Each had a pecan in its mouth but was not eating it! Instead, they were digging holes and burying the pecans to keep for their winter food supply.

The pecans were hidden under a thick cover of fallen leaves which presented no obstacle for these little critters. With their sharp claws, they quickly moved the leaves, dug a hole, and deposited their pecans. They had hit a gold mine! They were so busy burying their loot, they had not noticed me. I stared at them, waiting for the right moment to make my move.

The squirrels would hear me the second I started running through the thick leaves. While they were occupied digging a new hole, I saw my chance to strike and said to myself, steady, wait, wait....now!

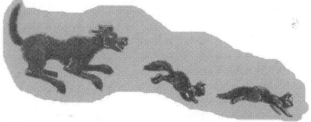

Off I ran just as fast as I could. Then one of the bushy-tailed creatures lunged onto a nearby tree. With the speed of an Olympic runner, he scampered up high to a safe spot. Assuming he would come down and not waste any time, I chased the other squirrel using only my three good legs.

Unfortunately, I slipped on a pile of leaves

wet from the morning dew. I got up fast and resumed my pursuit of the squirrel. But I failed to make the catch and watched in frustration as the second one made his getaway onto a tall pecan tree. Guess I had needed my injured leg more than I realized. Not to be totally humiliated, I barked and barked at the squirrel while he peered down at me from a high branch. After watching the squirrel for a long time, I gave up and left those two crafty characters in their safe havens.

It was a good thing there were still puddles of water from the rain, as I was thirsty, hot, tired, and panting after all that chasing. I lapped the water to quench my thirst and laid down in the mud. The mud felt cool to my tired, hot body. I turned over on my back and rolled around like a happy little pig.

Just as I was getting comfortable on my muddy bed, big bugs with wings began swirling around my head. I tried striking the bugs with my paw and shaking my head, but these pests were very persistent and had a bite that stung! My muddy bed must have been their home, because those pests made it quite clear I was not welcomed!

After several days without food, my strength was evaporating. I was discouraged, because I had not seen a person or house. How would I find a new home in this deserted place? Giving up hope was not a good option, so I decided to keep going. The woods made a safe place to walk while I searched for food. And the shade under the trees helped me feel cooler than out in the open under the sun.

After a while, I noticed mud was stuck all over my black fur and between the pads of my feet. I shook myself to loosen the mud as much as possible. Then, I laid down and rubbed my face and body with my paw. What I really needed was a good bath, but that would have to wait. With my teeth, I pulled at the clots of mud which tasted terrible.

I was wondering to myself what would happen next. The squirrels got away, I was attacked by big flying bugs that stung me, and I had not found anything to eat! It had been a really long day, and things seemed to be getting worse. Now it was dark again, and the sounds of the night were weird and scary. I heard animals moving around but could not see them. Thinking it could be those mean dogs, I began looking for a place to hide.

Chapter Four

Food at Last!

Since I was already in the woods, I thought about going back to the hollow log. But I was really tired and did not have enough strength to go any farther. Just then, I noticed some thick bushes. Putting my head down to keep my eyes from getting scratched, I pushed my way through the thick branches. That felt good against the side of my body, like someone was giving me a good brushing! It was a tight fit, but once I got through, there was a small open space between the bushes where I could lie down. The thick bushes made a good hideout. I felt safe, even though the night sounds still scared me.

Soon, I fell into a deep sleep and dreamed I was with a young boy. My tail was wagging as he hugged and petted me.

I was so happy. But, then, I heard a loud noise that awakened me. My dream had seemed so real, and I wished I was still being petted by that young boy. But now was not the time for wishing.

What was that loud noise? It sounded like whirring and whop, whop, whop! It got louder, as if it was nearly on top of me. I began to tremble. What should I do? If I ran out into the open, whatever it was might be able to see me. My best choice was to stay right where I was and hope the monster would go away. A ferocious wind caused thick dust to swirl all around me. Dust got in my ears, eyes, and nose. I closed my eyes and covered my head with my paws as much as possible, wishing this had been a bad dream. Suddenly, the sound was not so loud, the wind slowed down, and the dirt stopped swirling. For at least a minute, all was quiet. Then, I began to hear talking and was really curious about what was happening. It was time to muster my courage and investigate the situation without anyone seeing me. Ever so quietly, I crawled through the thick bushes and got close enough to see out, but where no one could see me. The voices I heard were Army soldiers! Where on earth was this place I had been left only a few days ago? Although I thought it had only been a few days, I was not really sure how long it had been.

Now, I could see what had made the loud sound. It was a huge helicopter! Soldiers filed out of the helicopter quickly one by one and gathered in one spot. One soldier, who must have been their leader, began speaking. I could not hear what he was saying but, after a few minutes, all the soldiers sat down and took something out of their large backpacks. My natural ability to detect scents left no doubt the soldiers had food. However, my fear kept me from getting any closer to them. I remained in hiding, hoping they might leave something for me to eat. Instinctively, I licked my mouth and started to drool! While I listened to the soldiers laughing and talking, I thought about ways I could get some of their food. All of a sudden, one of the soldiers stood up and started walking in my direction. When he got pretty close, I barked. He saw me!

I heard him shout to all the others, "Hey, there's a dog hiding in these bushes."

"Whistle to him, maybe he will come," the others shouted back. If they had only known how much I would have liked to come, but I was so frightened.

The soldier closest to me whistled and said, "Come here, I will feed you." But, I was trembling and did not move.

The leader of the group yelled, "Ok, get your gear! It is time to get moving." The soldiers gathered their gear and put it in their backpacks.

The one closest to me yelled to the others, "Hey, give me any food you have left. This poor dog looks like he is starving. At least we can leave him some food!" The soldier collected the food from the others and dropped a pile of their leftovers on the ground not far from me. As he was leaving, the soldier looked right at me and said, "We left food here to make you feel a little better. Sorry, I can't take you with me."

I watched as he ran off to join the others, unaware that would not be the last time I would see soldiers.

After they left, I came out and took a quick look around for any other animals that might have smelled the food. I wasted no time devouring the feast before me. The soldier left me beef jerky, cheese crackers, and other things that I had no idea what it was and did not even care. It was food that came just when I thought I might really be starving! I ate quickly but raised my head long enough to look for any other hungry creatures. Then, I ate every morsel.

Those soldiers probably saved my life, and now I could continue my search for a home. I wondered how long it would take to find a family who might want me. Maybe they would have a boy I could play with like the one in my dream.

Chapter Five

Signs of Hope

The food left by the soldiers came just when I was worried I might not survive much longer. Their kindness renewed my hope that I would find a family. I wondered what new adventure, danger, or challenge would happen today. Would I see the soldiers again? Were those wild dogs still lurking around to attack me? Hoping I would not see the dogs again, I decided to get going and see what would happen next. With my normal caution, I looked around and sniffed the air for any scents that would alert me to danger. I felt a lot better, even though my leg had not completely healed. My ears were still hurting and itching from the bites inflicted upon me by the big bugs. Nothing I tried relieved the itching and stinging; shaking my head or rubbing my ears with my paw did not work. So I tried to ignore the irritation and kept walking while it was still early in the morning.

Which way should I go? For certain, I was not going back where I came from; I could not go straight, because I saw a high fence ahead. Going left was not a good option, because the woods ended; without the protection of the woods, there would be no place to hide. To my right, the woods continued as far as I could see. Even though there were a few open spaces between some of the trees, the best way to go was still to the right. Before turning that way, I sniffed the air, noticing it seemed to have a fresher smell that day. For the first time since I had been abandoned on that dark night, I heard the sound of birds chirping and singing! Their sounds were not frightening; they made me feel happy. For another minute or two, I watched two birds flying from one tree to the next. They seemed to be playing with each other. I just had a feeling that something good would happen that day. There was a nice gentle breeze, which even felt cool and helped keep the flies and other bugs from bothering me. With my long tail high in the air, I turned right but stayed close to the edge of the woods in case I needed to make a quick getaway. I never knew what might happen, so I was very cautious.

That day, I even noticed the grass felt soft to my feet as I walked along. And I was more aware of other interesting things going on around me. Some really large birds with outstretched wings soared through the sky as if they were being carried by the wind. I also saw tiny birds moving their wings so incredibly fast I could hardly tell they had any, and their beaks were unusually long. These little birds made a humming sound as they flew up, down, and even sideways! One looked like it was standing still in mid-air while he stuck his tongue way out into the center of a flower. He must have liked whatever he tasted, because he stayed at the same flower long enough to eat all he wanted. I was fascinated by this little bird that hummed as he worked so hard to get food from each flower.

About that time, another one flew to the same spot. Maybe the two were friends. The first little bird did not want to share his flower, and he darted at the intruder full speed ahead, making a screeching sound. The intruding little bird knew he was not welcomed and quickly flew away to look for his own flowering bush.

Wishing it was as easy for me to find food as it seemed to be for them, I left the birds on their own and kept walking.

Later, I saw a car driving on the road next to the field where I was walking. I quickly moved closer to the woods and felt pretty certain no one in the car had seen me. But, at that very moment, the car slowed down and stopped.

A lady got out of the car and said, "Jonathan and Blake, stay in the car. I think I see a dog near the woods. He might need help." I did not know what to do. My thoughts were passing through my mind one after another. Could I trust her? Who were Jonathan and Blake? Would they feed me? The lady began walking in my direction, and I barked at her.

Then, she stopped and said, "Do not be afraid; I am not going to hurt you."

She continued walking closer to me. From the car I heard, "Mom, be careful, that is a big dog. He might try to bite you! Come back!" When she turned to answer them, I moved into the woods and positioned myself where they could no longer see me. The lady took the advice of those boys, who I assumed were her sons. She walked back to the car, got in, and drove away. Jonathan and Blake kept watching me as they drove away.

One of the boys seemed to be about the age of the boy in my dream. I wondered if I should have approached the lady. She was probably nice and seemed concerned about me. If I continued to be afraid of everyone, I might have to live alone for my whole life. That was not what I wanted!

That day had passed quickly. It was getting dark, my stomach was feeling empty again, and I was very tired. This place looked okay to sleep for the night, so I laid down and wondered about many things. Did I miss the chance to find a home? Should I have barked at that lady? Would her boys have liked me? Was I being too cautious? As I felt myself drifting into a deep sleep, I flashed back to the time I was dropped out of the back of the black truck. No wonder I was being cautious.

That night I dreamed that Jonathan and Blake were giving me treats and playing with me. It was so much fun. Maybe one day, it would not be a dream!

Chapter Six

More Soldiers and a Surprise!

Dreaming of Jonathan and Blake was much better than hearing barking dogs or other unidentified sounds. I woke up with a new outlook and was hopeful I might see them again. Sometimes, dreams do come true!

The next afternoon, I began hearing a faint sound that was different from the sounds an animal or helicopter makes. The sound was growing louder, so I perked my ears up to listen. I could hear voices singing in unison and decided to move to a spot where I could see them.

Could the singing be coming from a group of soldiers? Yes, it was!

There were soldiers running down the
road singing a funny song. The soldier at
the very back must have been the leader,
because he would sing first; then, all of
the other soldiers would repeat after him.
Their song went like this:

 "I want to be an Airborne Ranger,
Living a life of guts and danger.
Carry my rifle by my side,
In the sky, on the ground,
In the day, in the night.
Count on us! Airborne!"

All of a sudden I felt paralyzed with fear.
Airborne Rangers, YIKES! Those are tough
soldiers who parachute out of airplanes and
helicopters. Plus, they go to the most
dangerous places. That must be why they
sing about living on nothing but guts and
danger. Maybe I have been living on guts
and danger too. When I could no longer see
them, the sound of their singing faded away.
I was glad to see soldiers again, even though

I did not know if they were the same soldiers who had left food for me. However, I was certain I had been wandering around on an Army post. Surely there were more soldiers, helicopters, and no telling what else I might see.

My search had become an adventure, and I could only imagine how it might end. Feeling sort of dizzy from the excitement, plus the fact I had not eaten since the soldiers had given me food, I collapsed on the soft grass. My ear was hurting again but, since nothing had worked to give me relief, I tried not to think about it. I rolled over and rubbed my back on the soft grass which felt good but did not distract me from being hungry. If I was going to continue my search for a family, I had to find something to eat! It was still very hot, and those pesky bugs were swarming all around my head again. I felt too tired and weak to go any farther.

Just as I was getting very discouraged, I saw a house across the street. At first, I thought I might be dreaming. But then, I heard the garage door open, and a lady came

outside. I was in the middle of an open
field. All I could do was try to reach the
woods before the lady looked my way.

"Duchess! Come here!" the lady yelled.
Then she whistled, looking right at me! As
I was wondering who Duchess could be,
she whistled again and then said, "Oh my!
You're not Duchess!" With as much strength
as I could muster, I hopped along to the
woods where I was sure she could no longer
see me. When I looked back, she was gone.
Whew! That was scary! Feeling safe in the
thick cover provided by bushes and trees, I
laid down and wondered if the lady would
come out again.

In a few minutes, she appeared carrying a large bucket and a bowl. Where is she going? What is in the bucket and bowl? Then she began walking straight to where I was lying. Trembling with fear, I moved deeper into the woods where she would not see me. When the lady reached the edge of the woods, she stopped to place the bucket and bowl down on the ground. Then she walked back to the house and disappeared again.

The scent of food from the bowl reached me. I went to investigate, looking both ways each time I took a step. As I got closer, the smell of food was undeniable! My heart started to pound, and I hoped this was not a dream. I reached the bucket and peered inside to find cool fresh water. It was more water than I could drink! Nothing had ever tasted so good. I lapped the water for a long time before stopping to see what was in the bowl. But, as soon as I did, it took me no time to gobble up every morsel of food. I had forgotten how great it felt to have a full tummy and wanted to howl with delight. Instead, not making a sound, I returned to the woods.

The food had given me much needed strength, and it tasted so good! Now, I was determined to camp out at this spot, hoping the lady would bring me more food the next day. Nothing disturbed my sleep that night!

Chapter Seven

The Lady and Duchess

Early the next morning, the lady walked out to the field. To my surprise, a black lab was walking with her. Umm, could that be Duchess?

Sure enough, I heard the lady yell, "Hey, Duchess, don't go into those woods. Come back here right now!"

No wonder the lady had whistled to me the day before. Duchess was a black lab who looked a lot like me.

When the lady called her, Duchess stopped and turned around. Without hesitating, she ran back to the lady. Duchess was one lucky dog, and she had a nice lady taking care of her. They kept walking up and down the field while I stayed hidden in the woods.

Then, the lady walked over to the bucket and bowl she had left the day before and told Duchess that all the food was gone. Duchess was scurrying around with her nose to the ground. No doubt, she had picked up my scent. She would have found me, but the lady turned around and walked back across the field. It was easy to see that Duchess was very attached to the lady because, instead of following my scent, she ran to the lady and walked by her side back to their house. Could I dare hope that I might have found a home at last?

As they were walking, I heard another lady call out, "Aubrey, I heard you took food to the dog that Jonathan, Blake, and I saw a couple of days ago." So Aubrey was the name of the kind lady bringing me food and water.

Aubrey answered, "Hi, Mary Jo. You heard right! I was just checking to see if the poor

dog had eaten the food I left for him."
This was starting to make sense to me.
These two ladies were friends. Aubrey
continued her conversation with Mary Jo,
and I listened to them talk about how sad
and scared I looked. Aubrey told Mary Jo
all about how she had seen me in the field
the day before and, at first glance, she had
thought I was Duchess. Then Aubrey
realized I must be the lost dog that Mary Jo,
Jonathan, Blake, and other neighbors had
seen. Aubrey continued telling Mary Jo
how she had taken water and food to me,
then returned to her house and watched to
see if I would come out to drink the water
and eat the food.

Aubrey said, "Mary Jo, I got a long look
at that dog; he is terribly thin and close to
starving! I think he must have belonged to
someone, because he has on a blue collar. I
am certain that he is still in the woods,
hoping I will bring him more food and
water."

"Aubrey," interrupted Mary Jo, "I hope
you and General McFarren want another dog

because, if you continue to feed that dog, he will not leave."

"No, no," Aubrey said. "We have Duchess plus our two cats, Mittens and Pretty Boy. I just want to catch this poor dog before he starves. Then, I will call the post Military Police. Surely, they can find a home for him, because he really is a beautiful dog."

Mary Jo answered, "But he looks like he will need a lot of veterinary care. You really think someone will adopt him? Oops, it is getting late. I have to go. Jonathan and Blake will be coming home from school soon. Do you mind if they come and help you take fresh food and water out to the dog?"

Aubrey replied, "Oh. That would be great, because dogs seem to be more at ease with kids. I think your boys could help a lot. Tell them that I have the Popsicles they like."

Had Mary Joe said General McFarren? Could Aubrey's husband be a general? Aubrey said she was going to call the Military Police once she caught me! A general's wife calling the Military Police. That did not sound good. I did not know whether to stay or keep moving, but I had fresh food and water every day. At least I needed to stay until I was stronger.

Chapter Eight

The Boy in My Dream

Aubrey is a nice lady; perhaps the general is a pretty good guy. I decided to stay, and everything was quiet for a while. I kept hiding near the edge of the woods and began to wonder what a Popsicle might be. It would not be long before I would find out.

Later that day, I saw two boys riding their bikes on the street, and they were talking about me! I could hear them say their mom told them Miss Aubrey had Popsicles. They talked about how they were going to help her take fresh food and water to the dog hiding in the woods. The boys got off their bikes and went up to Aubrey's back door.

She came out holding something in each hand and said, "Hi, Jonathan and Blake. Your mom told me that you would be coming, so I have a Popsicle for each of you. Here, Jonathan. I remember you like cherry ones. And Blake, here is your favorite flavor, lemon. Would you like to help me take fresh water and food to the dog hiding in the woods? I am certain this is the same dog you saw just the other day."

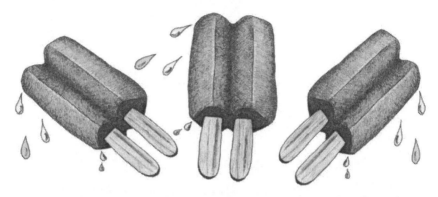

So Jonathan might have been the boy I dreamed about, and he has a little brother, Blake. Both of them walked with Aubrey across the field toward me. Jonathan carried a container of fresh water, and Blake carried a bag with fresh dog food. They asked Aubrey lots of questions. Will the dog bite us? Have you petted him? What is his name? Are you going to catch him and call the Military Police to come get him? All of their questions confused me.

After adding the fresh water to my bucket and food to my bowl, they peered into the woods trying to see me. I thought about walking out to them. Just then, Jonathan whistled and called to me with a kind and reassuring voice.

I really wanted to go to him but did not have enough courage. I waited patiently, watching until they left and walked back to Aubrey's house.

Now, I knew why the boys liked Popsicles. They had each broken off a piece and dropped it on the ground by my bowl of food. They must have known that I was hoping to try a bite of that cold, icy treat!

Happiness filled my heart as I thought about Aubrey, Jonathan, and Blake. Even though my ear still hurt, it felt great to have plenty of food and water! After those two days, I was really feeling hopeful about my future! Would I be adopted by Aubrey and get to play with Duchess? Maybe Jonathan and Blake would want me to be their dog! Oh, so much to think about. I wondered what would happen next.

That night, I curled up in my favorite spot in the safety of the woods but not far from my water bucket and food bowl. This was now my area, and I was going to defend it against any intruders. The daily supply of food and water had given me much needed strength. I was feeling so much better, and even brave. However, I did not know my new bravery would soon be tested. At least for another week, things went very well. Without fail, Aubrey faithfully brought fresh water and food each day.

Duchess always came along with her, but one thing changed. Aubrey left the bucket of water in the same spot, but she began moving my food bowl a little farther into the open field. I did not like having to leave the woods to reach my food, because that put me in view of other animals. Every day, I looked carefully before walking out in the field to the bowl of food. If I waited too long, some other animal might see my food. Like me, most animals would only go into an open field during the night. I had to be brave and get to the food before dark.

I was not expecting any other creatures, except those dogs, to eat my food. But the next day, I discovered hundreds of ants all over my food! I never thought something so tiny would steal my food! Since I did not want to eat ants, I returned to my spot in the woods, hoping Aubrey would notice the ants and solve this huge problem!

Chapter Nine

Problem Solved

When Aubrey and Duchess walked out the next day with fresh food, they discovered the hundreds of tiny ants crawling all over my bowl.

She said, "Oh no, Duchess, look at the ants. We must do something!" Duchess was running around with her nose to the ground. I knew she had picked up my scent again and was trying to find me. But Aubrey was whistling for her, and Duchess followed her back to the house. Umm, what would happen next? No dog, even a very hungry one, would want to eat food with ants crawling all over it! Well, would you? I was happy Aubrey had seen the ants, and I knew she would find a solution.

In a few minutes, she was walking with a bucket toward the ant-infested food. The boys had come with her. Jonathan carried a large pan, and Blake had a paper bag. I watched from the woods to see what would happen. When Aubrey reached the bowl, she turned the bucket down, pouring water over the ants. All the ants were washed away, and the bowl was clean. What would keep the ants from coming back? Aubrey already thought of that possibility. Jonathan placed the pan on the ground. Aubrey poured water into the pan and placed the clean bowl in the center of the water. Blake opened the bag he was carrying and turned it upside down over the bowl. I smelled the fresh food falling into the bowl. As the scent of the food reached me, I barked to get their attention. It worked, because all three of them turned their heads in my direction. I believe they understood I was trying to say thank you for coming to my rescue! Now my bowl was protected by a water moat. If an ant tried to get into the pan, it would drown before stealing my food.

I heard Aubrey say, "Good job, boys! Would you like a Popsicle?" It made me happy to watch the boys run to Aubrey's house to receive their reward!

As soon as they were out of sight, I moved quickly to the bowl of food and ate very fast. Just as I turned to run back to the woods, I saw one of those mean dogs drinking from my water bucket. He must have seen me eating. He began growling and showing his teeth to scare me.

The mean dog thought I would leave my hiding place, and he would make it his own place. I knew he would fight with me if I stayed. Plus, those other dogs might be lurking around waiting for a chance to eat my food. There was no time to think about what to do. I had to act now! I was so thankful he was more interested in drinking the water than chasing me, and I was able to escape before he could attack me.

"Hey, come here. Run fast!" Jonathan yelled at me. Then he told Blake, "Hurry. Go get Miss Aubrey!"

Blake ran to the house but, before he got there, Aubrey came out. Jonathan wanted to help me, so I ran toward him. Once again, I was hesitant to get closer to Jonathan. I stopped a few yards before reaching him. We stared at each other while we watched Blake and Aubrey run to us.

Once there, Aubrey said, "I think that mean dog has left. He was probably frightened when he saw us coming."

Now, what was I going to do? I stood still and wagged my tail. They knew I was beginning to trust them, and their voices made me feel safe. Jonathan took a few steps toward me.

Aubrey said, "Don't go any closer. The dog has been really frightened and needs to know we will not hurt him." They slowly walked away. I watched as they returned to Aubrey's house.

It was almost dark, and I did not know if the mean dog was really gone; he might still be lurking around. Therefore, I decided to sleep under some big bushes right next to Aubrey's house. I felt really safe and slept like a baby all night. Early the next morning, I was awakened by a meow, meow. It was the sound of a cat.

At first I thought I was dreaming again, but then, I heard Aubrey's voice. I realized I had been sleeping right next to her screened-in porch. I could see inside the porch without being seen. Aubrey came out to the porch and sat down in a white rocking chair. Duchess followed and laid down by Aubrey's feet. I heard the cat meow, meow again.

Aubrey said, "Duchess, I think Mittens and Pretty Boy must be telling us they are hungry." If Aubrey and the General have two cats, a gray and white one named Mittens and a larger, fluffy black cat named Pretty Boy, they must like pets! But what was the chance of them wanting another pet? Could I win their hearts so Aubrey would not call the Military Police? My heart pounded. Somehow, they have to want me to be in their family. (50)

Chapter Ten

Irresistible

I was learning a little more about General McFarren. First, he is Aubrey's husband. Did I mention his name is Freddy? Don't you think a general named Freddy must be okay? Almost every day, I watched General Freddy arrive home from work in his red Chevy hot rod. That was another clue he was not your ordinary general. He was always happy to see Aubrey, Duchess, Mittens, and Pretty Boy. Most evenings, they all sat out on the porch, and sometimes I watched them play together.

One day, he asked Aubrey a funny question, "Did you see the stranger in the woods today?" Stranger in the woods, what did he mean? I spent a lot of time in the woods, and I had not seen a stranger. This was an Army post; there were soldiers everywhere. How could a stranger be in the woods? After listening to Aubrey's answer, I realized General Freddy was talking about me! I was the stranger in the woods General Freddy wanted to know more about. And, I never heard him say he did not want to keep me. I thought General Freddy had never seen me, but I heard him tell Aubrey about the day he saw me while he was jogging. He described how thin I was and wondered if I would survive. He said he even whistled to me; but I ran away, disappeared into the woods, and he had not seen me again. So General Freddy actually saw me even before Aubrey did.

Remember those soldiers I saw running that day? Well, I still saw them every morning running by General Freddy and Aubrey's house singing that funny song. All of a sudden, I realized that General Freddy might be the commander of those soldiers!

Wow! Every day was getting more and more interesting! Since I had been living in the woods across the street from their house, I had been watching General Freddy leave at dawn and return at dusk in his red Chevy hot rod. Later, I learned he only drove a short distance every morning to an airfield where he boarded a helicopter and was flown to work. He told Aubrey about seeing alligators on the edge of the river as he flew high above them. Wild dogs were one thing to fear, but alligators? Yikes! Trust me. I am not making this up! However, I did think it would be fun to ride in the helicopter or alongside General Freddy in his red Chevy hot rod!

The next morning, I decided to nap in the open field. But I stayed close to the woods in case I needed to hide quickly. The mean dogs had not returned. I wondered if they had heard this was where General Freddy lived and decided not to create any trouble. Since I was not as fearful of them anymore, I went to sleep and did not notice Aubrey walking across the field in my direction. But, as she got closer to me, I heard the sound of her footsteps and woke up. When she saw me raise my head, Aubrey began speaking to me in a soft, gentle voice. I knew her voice and was not afraid. However, I did not want her to call the Military Police; so I began walking to the woods.

Immediately, Aubrey sat down on the

ground in front of me. That helped me feel at ease. Besides, I could smell something good she was holding in her hand. Aubrey was far enough away that she could not reach out to touch me but close enough to toss me a piece of whatever she was holding in her hand. The smell of food caused any fear I had to melt away. Just then, Aubrey tossed a piece of something that landed a few feet in front of me. I walked closer to see what smelled so irresistible. Now, I could grab the small bite of meat. It tasted so good! Aubrey tossed another piece to draw me even closer to her. Her plan worked. I snatched another bite and found myself within touching distance of Aubrey.

She said, "Come on now. You know me. I have been feeding you for a long time." Then Aubrey held a piece of the meat in the palm of her hand. I walked a little closer and took the piece from her outstretched hand. With her other hand, Aubrey quickly snapped a leash to my collar. Oh no! I panicked! What is going to happen? I tried to back away, but Aubrey had a good grip on the leash. She stood up quickly, continued talking softly to me, and started walking back to the house.

As we walked, Aubrey patted my head, reassuring me I was going to be safe with her. When we got to the house, we went inside the screened-in porch. Aubrey removed the leash, and she went into the house. As I sat alone on her porch, I felt really relieved that she finally caught me. Quickly, Aubrey came back with a bowl of food. She sat down in the rocking chair and placed the bowl on the floor. My tail was wagging so fast, which showed Aubrey I was very happy! I ate the food as though I had not had any food for a month. Aubrey had been feeding me every day, but I was still very skinny!

I needed to tell Aubrey how much I wanted to be her dog! So after I ate the last bite of food, I sat down beside her, gently placed my paw on her leg, and licked her hand. This was my way of saying, thank you! Please let me stay with your family.

Aubrey said, "I am so sorry you can't stay with me, but you are going to be given to a nice family." Then, she went inside and called the Military Police to come pick me up. I was very sad. Aubrey seemed sad too. The Military Police came quickly and loaded me in the back of their enclosed truck. There was no way I could get out. I was scared.

Aubrey asked the Military Police, "How long will it take to find a family for this dog?" I could not hear what was said, but Aubrey did not like their answer.

She told the Military Police, "I have changed my mind. Take him out." They opened the door of the truck, and I jumped out. I was so happy to watch them drive away.

Aubrey said to me, "If you're going to stay here, the first thing we must do is give you a bath. You are very dirty!" Did you know a dog can grin? I was grinning from ear to ear! A bath would be wonderful. I could hardly wait! Aubrey called Mary Jo to come help bathe me. Jonathan and

Blake also came, and they were very excited. My wagging tail again showed how happy and relieved I was. The boys rubbed my head while Aubrey used a garden hose and let water run all over me. All of them talked about how many ticks and fleas covered my body! Mary Jo poured shampoo on my fur, making certain not to miss a spot. I could have stood there forever. It felt so good! While gently scrubbing my body with shampoo, they started to giggle and laugh. Jonathan and Blake got as wet as I did. It was a hot day, and they could not resist spraying each other with the hose. After a good final rinse, I shook hard to dry myself. Then, Aubrey draped a large towel over me, and the boys took turns rubbing my fur. I was no longer afraid and didn't even cry out when Aubrey cleaned my smelly, aching ear. That was not easy, because the ointment she used stung!

"Look! Here comes General Freddy in his red Chevy," the boys yelled. As he turned onto the driveway, Jonathan and

Blake ran over to his car. They could hardly wait to tell him Miss Aubrey finally caught the stranger in the woods! General Freddy got out of his car and began walking over to me. I felt a little afraid but did not bark. I showed General Freddy respect by standing quietly at attention. To my surprise, he slowly approached me and knelt down on one knee.

Then with kindness, General Freddy said, "There now, you are a handsome dog. I know you have been afraid for a long time." He patted my head and said, "You are safe now." Unable to contain myself any longer, I licked the General's face; and everyone began laughing. I had never had so much fun!

Chapter Eleven

What's a Veterinarian?

General Freddy brought a big dog cage to the porch.

He said, "This will make a fine place for you to sleep tonight. Tomorrow, we will take you to the veterinarian. He will examine you to determine if you need any special care. You are still very thin, and your ear looks infected."

Umm. A veterinarian, is that a doctor for a dog? I did not like this plan, but I trusted Aubrey and General Freddy. They put a soft blanket in the dog cage and bowls of food and water nearby. Before going into the house, Aubrey and General Freddy both petted me. I went into the cage and laid down on the soft, clean blanket. That was the best bed I ever had. I curled myself into a tight ball. In no time, I was sound asleep.

The next thing I heard was Aubrey saying, "Good morning, are you ready to see the veterinarian?" As soon as I heard her voice, I stood up, stretched, and walked out of the cage.

Aubrey reached down, hugged me, and said, "Don't worry, I am going to take you. Everything will be okay." General Freddy had gone to work. So, it was just Aubrey and me going to the dog doctor. Aubrey attached a leash to my collar, walked me to her car, opened the back door, and told me to jump in. Aubrey had fed me for a month, bathed me, and given me a place to sleep. So I did what she said.

On the way, I whimpered in fear because I did not know what to expect. Aubrey kept saying, "You're okay. Everything will be fine." I believed her.

The veterinarian was kind and gentle as he looked at my ears. Then he examined my whole body and told Aubrey I was in pretty bad shape and very lucky to be rescued. He said I needed medicine for my ear and other things that I did not understand. But he thought I should be fine now that I had been adopted by a loving family who would take good care of me. ADOPTED! I knew what that meant. We left the veterinary clinic, and my tail wagged all the way home!

When we arrived home, Aubrey said, "The porch is going to be your room for a while. The doctor said you need to have an area by yourself so you can get plenty of rest. But it won't be long before you will be playing with Duchess, Mittens, and Pretty Boy." I was very content to have my own room, cozy bed, and a good view of the woods where I had hidden for a month.

Whenever she took Duchess for a walk, Aubrey would bring her over to the porch to see me but only through the screen. Mary Jo, Jonathan, and Blake also came by to see me. The boys knew they had to wait until I was better before they could play with me. Slowly, I gained much needed weight, and my ear healed. Oh, I almost forgot! Aubrey and General Freddy had given me my own name. You must surely know they named me Stranger!

One morning, General Freddy and Aubrey opened the door, and Duchess came out on the porch. Our tails began to wag as we sniffed each other with our noses. That is how dogs communicate. General Freddy opened the door to the backyard, and Duchess ran outside. I turned and looked at Aubrey.

She said, "Go ahead, Stranger. Follow Duchess. It is okay." So out I went, chasing after Duchess. We had so much fun! Duchess ran circles around me, then she would stop and reverse directions. She was very fast. I had never had so much fun!

The next day, I met Mittens and Pretty Boy. As you would expect, we approached each other with much more caution than Duchess and I had the day before. Pretty Boy, the black and white cat, came over to me first. He meowed, rubbed against my leg, and began to purr! Instinctively, I knew that meant he liked me! After a few minutes, Mittens, the smaller gray and white cat, walked over to me. She was more timid than Pretty Boy. So, I waited until she could tell I was not going to hurt her. After all, I was a dog, and she was a cat! I laid down and rested my head on my front legs. This position was far less scary to a little cat. Slowly, Mittens got close enough to sniff my paws. Guess what? She started licking my ear, which tickled me!

But I stayed still, not wanting to startle her. She knew my ear was still healing, and she was treating it the best way she knew how.

I had passed the final test to become a full member of this family! Everyone had now given me the stamp of approval! Yippee! That night was different from all the other nights. I no longer slept on the porch.

To my surprise, Aubrey opened the door to the house and said, "Come on in, Stranger.

It is time for you to sleep inside with the rest of the family." So, without hesitating, I walked inside. Duchess, Mittens, and Pretty Boy showed me around the house.

Then Aubrey said, "Time to go to bed. Come let me show you where you will be sleeping." I followed Duchess as we walked down the hall into a room where there were two large round dog beds right beside each other. Immediately, Duchess laid down on one of the beds. Puzzled, I looked up at Aubrey.

She said, "Go ahead, Stranger. It is okay. The other bed is for you." This was too good to be true, but it was true. I quickly laid down on the other bed. Then, I looked at Duchess just in time to watch Mittens curling up next to her! Yes, a cat curling up next to a dog! After a few minutes, here came Pretty Boy. Yep, you guessed it, Pretty Boy curled up next to me!

I laid very still until I was certain they were all asleep. Then I put my head down and fell into a deep, wonderful sleep. My dream of having a loving home became true. It was more than I could have ever wished or imagined. Now I was the happiest dog on earth!

Chapter Twelve

Happy Ending

Every good story must end. But before this one does, I must tell you about my great adventure with Duchess!

I had stayed very close to the house, having no interest in wandering anymore. General Freddy or Aubrey always let Duchess and me go outside every night before we went to sleep. Duchess had been begging me to take her on a personal tour of the places I had traveled. This was back when I was known as the stranger in the woods, an abandoned dog living on his own. I had always said no to Duchess until this one night. It was a beautiful night, the moon was full, and there was not a cloud in the sky. General Freddy would always say those were perfect conditions for a parachute jump. I understood why, because the cloudless night sky and full moon would help anyone see much better. So I decided to surprise Duchess that night.

We went out as usual but, this time, I was

the first one out the door. When Duchess came out, I turned in a circle excitedly and then took off running fast. Somehow, Duchess knew what I had planned. She quickly caught up to me, and we kept running with our noses in the air and our ears pushed back by the wind. It felt exhilarating. Then I made a sudden turn, and Duchess stayed right with me. I was heading to the spot where I had been dropped out by the man in the black truck. When we got there, I told Duchess how lonely and afraid I felt as I watched the truck drive away. We continued running from place to place, stopping long enough at each spot for me to tell Duchess about every adventure. Duchess learned about my hard fall out of the truck and about my daily search for food, water, and a place to sleep.

She saw the hollow log where I had hidden from the wild dogs and had the close encounter with the squirrels. Of course, I took Duchess to the spot I had been scared half to death by the helicopter and told her about the soldiers who had been so kind to leave food for me. Duchess listened with amazement, and I know she wondered how I had survived. We continued walking to the place Mary Jo, Jonathan, and Blake had first seen me. Hours passed before we finally got back to the woods where Aubrey had brought me water and food. I told Duchess how I had watched her and Aubrey every day for a whole month and about my yearning for them to become my family.

By the time we got back to the house, we were both exhausted and muddy from our exciting adventure. General Freddy and Aubrey were waiting for us.

"Where in the world have you been?" they asked. We leaned our heads to one side trying to look very innocent. I have no doubt that General Freddy and Aubrey knew exactly what we had been doing!

That night, we were too dirty to go inside, so we had a slumber party on the back porch with Mittens and Pretty Boy. Of course, we told our feline siblings all about our adventure before going to sleep in our normal positions, Pretty Boy next to me and Mittens next to Duchess. That was a night Duchess and I would never forget.

In the years ahead, there were many other great adventures. We lived at West Point (home of the U.S. Military Academy), Egypt (yes, where the pyramids are), Fort Riley (home of the Calvary), and, finally, the great state of Texas. Maybe one day, I will tell you about everything that happened to us in each of those places.

I had spent many nights in those lonely woods, hoping and dreaming of belonging to a family. But I never thought, even in my wildest imagination, my life would become the most wonderful adventure any dog could ever experience. I can honestly say I lived HAPPILY EVER AFTER!

About the Author

Aubrey and her husband, Freddy (Lieutenant General, US Army, retired), live in the Texas hill country. Their life has been an interesting journey, living in many places during Freddy's thirty-seven years of service in the United States Army. Their pets have always been close members of their family and enjoyed many adventures moving from place to place. This book is based on the true account of how an abandoned, hurt dog met Aubrey and joined their family.

♡ Aubrey and Freddy with Stranger and Duchess ♡

About the Artist

Jennifer Medeiros holds a degree in Sports Science, Kinesiology, and Bio-Mechanics, with a minor in Nutrition. She has been an artist for many years and has won awards for several of her works. Born and raised in Marin County, California, she loves animals, art, and sports, especially figure skating. She was a Professional skater with Holiday On Ice, Ice Follies, and Advanced Entertainment. Currently she is a USFS skating judge.

The Use of Popsicle(s)

Popsicle is a copyright- used under - fair use. Under the United States law as described: fair use is a limitation and exception to the exclusive right granted by the copyright law to an author of creative work. In United States copyright law, fair use is a doctrine that permits limited use of copyrighted material without acquiring permission from the rights holders. Examples of fair use include commentary, search engines, criticism, parody, news reporting, research, teaching, library archiving and scholarships. It provides for the legal unlicensed citation or incorporation of copyrighted material in another author's work under a four-factor balancing test.

Made in the USA
Columbia, SC
09 February 2024

31167146R00046